Gower College Swansea

Sheridan Morley, *Spectator*

'Ridley is a singular writer, a prolific polymath, probably a
genius, and the creator of some of the most peculiar,
grotesque and compelling B films) of the last
several years.'

Philip Ridley was born in the East End of London, where he still lives and works. He studied painting at St Martin's School of Art and has exhibited widely throughout Europe. As a writer his credits include *Crocodilia* (1988), *In The Eyes of Mr Fury* (1989), *Flamingoes in Orbit* (1990), and four novels for children; *Mercedes Ice* (1989), *Dakota of the White Flats* (1989), *Krindlekrax* (1991), winner of the Smarties Prize for Children's Fiction and the W. H. Smith Mind Boggling Books Award, and *Meteorite Spoon* (1994). His plays for BBC Radio are *October Scars the Skin* (1989), *The Aquarium of Coincidences* (1989) and *Shambolic Rainbow* (1991). His two short films – *Visiting Mr Beak* (1987) and *The Universe of Dermot Finn* (1988) – were soon followed by his highly acclaimed screenplay for *The Krays* (1990), winner of the Evening Standard Best Film of the Year Award, and his debut feature film as both writer and director, the controversial *The Reflecting Skin* (1990), which won eleven international awards, was voted one of the Best Ten Films of 1991 by the 'L.A. Times' and prompted 'Rolling Stones Magazine' to describe him as "a visionary". In 1991 he was awarded the Most Promising Newcomer to British Film at the Evening Standard Film Awards. His first stage play, the award winning *The Pitchfork Disney*, was premiered at the Bush Theatre in London in 1991. His second stage play, *The Fastest Clock in the Universe* was premiered at the Hampstead Theatre the following year and went on to win the Meyer-Whitworth Prize, a Time Out Award, and both the Critics Circle and the Evening Standard Award for most Promising Playwright. Incidentally, this is the first time the Evening Standard has given the Most Promising Award to the same person twice, for both film and theatre. His work has been translated into sixteen languages, including Japanese. *Ghost From A Perfect Place* is his third stage play.

Philip Ridley

Ghost from a Perfect Place

Methuen Drama

Methuen Drama Modern Play

First published in Great Britain in 1994 by Methuen Drama

ISBN–0–413–68860–7

A CIP catalogue record for this book
is available at the British Library

Front cover is taken from the poster for the play.
Cover concept Scars Davies, photograph by Malcolm Russel.

Phototypeset by Wilmaset Ltd, Birkenhead, Wirral

For my friend
Tom Yuill
1965–1993
– love is never lost.

'What kind of depravity would you not bring about
in order to root out depravity forever?
Yes, submerge us in filth
and embrace the executioner.
But transform the world.
It needs it!'

Brecht

'Few things are sadder than the truly monstrous.'

Nathanael West

'The fire is out at the heart of the world:
all tame creatures have grown up wild.'

Andrew Motion

Ghost from a Perfect Place was premièred at the Hampstead Theatre, London on 7 April 1994, with the following cast:

Torchie Sparks	Bridget Turner
Travis Flood	John Wood
Rio Sparks	Trevyn McDowell
Miss Sulphur	Rachel Power
Miss Kerosene	Katie Tyrrell

Directed by Matthew Lloyd
Designer Laurie Dennett
Lighting Robert Bryan

Artistic Director for Hampstead Theatre Jenny Topper

Act One

A dimly lit room in Bethnal Green, the East End of London. There has been a fire sometime in the past: the walls, floor and woodwork are all badly scorched. A table, two hard-backed chairs, sink, gas oven – everything bears signs of the blaze. One window reveals a pitch-black night beyond. Two doors: one leading to a bedroom, the other to a wooden landing and stairs leading down, presumably to street.

Torchie *is sitting on chair. She is sixty years old, but looks older. She is wearing a black petticoat. Her hair is long and very grey, almost white.*

Beside **Torchie** *are a pair of black shoes and a wooden walking-stick. A black velvet dress decorated with gold brocade hangs over back of other chair.*

Torchie *is just finishing wrapping her left leg in a crêpe bandage.*

Pause.

A knock on the door.

Torchie *glances at door.*

Pause.

Another knock.

Torchie (*calling*) Who is it?

Pause.

Another knock.

Torchie, *her leg now bandaged, picks up walking-stick and limps to door.*

Torchie (*calling*) Who is it?

Travis (*off-stage*) Who are you?

Torchie Who am I? I live here. What do you want?

Travis I'm looking for a girl called Rio.

Torchie That's my granddaughter.

Travis She asked me to meet her here.

Torchie She's not here yet.

Travis I'll come in and wait, then.

Torchie Lor'struth . . . well, yes. Give me a second. I'm not decent. I'll call when it's safe. You hear me? I'll call when it's safe.

Travis Yes, yes.

Torchie *goes back to chair, picks up shoes, then goes into bedroom.*

Torchie (*calling, off-stage from bedroom*) Safe now!

Travis *enters. He is sixty years old but could pass for younger. He has a strong, solid appearance and is wearing a black, shot-silk, single-breasted suit, white shirt (with gold cuff-links), black tie (with gold tie-pin) and black leather shoes. There is a white silk handkerchief protruding from the top pocket of his jacket and a white lily in his lapel. His hair is dyed very black, thick and neatly cut. In his left hand he is holding a bunch of white lilies.*

Travis *closes door behind him.*
He looks at the burnt room.

Torchie (*off-stage, from bedroom*) You in yet?

Travis Yes.

Pause.

Torchie (*from bedroom*) Rio usually arranges to meet her men visitors while I'm out. You must be early.

Travis Not by much.

Torchie (*from bedroom*) Lor'struth! I've forgotten my dress! That's your fault, disturbing my routine. Can you see it? Over the back of the chair.

Travis Yes.

Torchie (*from bedroom*) Pass it in to me, will you?

Travis *picks up dress and approaches bedroom.*

Torchie *holds out walking-stick from bedroom.*

Torchie (*from bedroom*) No peeking now.

Travis *puts dress on walking-stick. Walking-stick and dress disappear into bedroom.*

Travis *continues looking at the scorched room.*

Pause.

Torchie (*from bedroom*) You been with Rio before?

Travis No.

Torchie (*from bedroom*) When did you meet her?

Travis This afternoon.

Torchie (*from bedroom*) Met her in the graveyard did you?

Travis Yes.

Torchie (*from bedroom*) She's always there. You go to the graveyard much?

Travis No.

Torchie (*from bedroom*) You can see it from the window. Have a look.

Travis *goes to the window and looks out.*

Torchie Not exactly the cheeriest of views, is it?

Travis *gets a little soot on the cuff of his shirt from the window-frame. He tuts irritably and tries – not altogether successfully – to brush it off.*

Torchie (*from bedroom*) You lost someone?

Travis What?

Torchie (*from bedroom*) Being in the graveyard.

Travis No. I used to live round here. Years ago. I'm back on a visit.

Torchie (*from bedroom*) Seeing how many friends have dropped dead.

Travis Something like that! When I got here, though, I realised I'd forgotten most of them anyway. Everyone just blurs into one nameless face after a while.

Slight pause.

Torchie (*from bedroom*) Easy to forget.

Travis People remember me, though. They've been stopping me all day. Reminding me of the day I shook their hand or called them by their first name. Then they tell me what they've been doing since I've been gone. Very boring.

Torchie (*from bedroom*) What's that?

Travis Other people's stories have never interested me much.

Torchie *enters.*
She is wearing the black dress with gold brocade and the black shoes. She sits at table and starts putting on make-up – pale powder, bright red lipstick, black eyeliner: everything a little too heavy. She barely glances at **Travis**.

Torchie You'll be gone by the time I get back, I hope.

Slight pause.

Let me give you a word of advice. Don't mess with Rio. One of her men visitors tried to get away without paying a few weeks ago and I found one of his fingernails in the floorboards. So you treat Rio properly. Hear me?

Travis Don't you know who I am?

Torchie *gives* **Travis** *a quick look then continues with make-up.*

Torchie No.

Travis How long have you lived in the East End?

Torchie All my life, for my sins.

Travis Look again.

Torchie *looks at* **Travis**.

Pause.

Travis *smells the lily in his lapel.*

Slowly, a cry of surprise forms at the back of **Torchie***'s throat.*

She stands.

The cry gets louder and louder.

Travis *smiles, enjoying it.*

Torchie Travis Flood!

Travis In the flesh.

Torchie Lor'struth! Mr Flood! How can you ever forgive me?

Travis I don't know.

Torchie Mr Travis Flood! You haven't been in these parts since . . .

Travis Nineteen sixty-nine.

Torchie Yes. It must be. That's when they were arresting all the gangsters.

Travis Don't say gangster! I was not a gangster! Someone said it to me this afternoon and I lashed out. Broke his nose and robbed him of a few teeth I shouldn't wonder. He won't call me gangster again in a hurry. So . . . no, I was not a gangster. I offered a service. That's all. I was a . . . a business man.

Slight pause.

Torchie Well, they were certainly arresting a lot of business men in nineteen sixty-nine.

Travis That's why I got away.

Torchie Got away with everything, I'd say –

Travis I didn't mean it like that –

Torchie But you deserved to get away, Mr Flood. The service you offered was a much needed one. The streets were safe to walk then, day or night. A lot's changed since then.

Travis I can see that. I hardly recognised the place.
Everything smashed and broken. No order. It's like a
wasteland. When I used to be here, you could swim in the
canal. Now it's nothing but a sewer. And the graffiti . . . we
never used words like that in the heydays. Disgraceful! In
the graveyard, I saw some children putting a dead rat in the
hands of a stone angel. And the kids were filthy too. Pale as
ghosts. Zombies. That's what everyone looks like now.
Zombies. Where's everyone's self-respect gone? Look at the
state of this place. I ask you, what have you all become since
I've been gone?

Pause.

Torchie Oh, Mr Flood . . . you . . . you make me feel
ashamed. Really you do.

Pause.

At least . . . at least I'm wearing my gladrags and warpaint.
Hope that helps de-zombiefy me a little.

Travis A little.

Torchie You look a vision, though, Mr Flood. Can I say
that? You look the same now as you did in the . . . in the
heydays, to use your word. You look a million dollars.

Travis Don't undersell me. That's practically the price of
this suit alone.

Torchie Silk is it, Mr Flood?

Travis Shot-silk, yes.

Torchie I adore the feel of silk.

Slight pause.

Travis (*holding out arm*) Have a stroke.

Torchie Oh, I don't like to, Mr Flood.

Travis I'd like you to.

Gingerly, **Torchie** *steps forward, and touches* **Travis***'s sleeve.*

Torchie Oh, it's divine, Mr Flood. That's the only word for it. You know what you've got, Mr Flood? Pizzazz! Pizzazz by the bucket load and no mistake. They broke the mould when they made you. The mould marked pizzazz was smashed for ever.

Pause.

Mr Flood . . . do you remember me?

Slight pause.

Travis No.

Torchie We used to speak, Mr Flood.

Travis I spoke to everyone.

Torchie I had long black hair in those days. And a beautiful figure, so I was told.

Travis Well, your hair's still long at any rate.

Torchie Let me give you a clue, Mr Flood. Every Saturday night!

Travis Every Saturday night?

Torchie That's when you and your boys would visit us. Me and my husband. Ring any bells?

Travis Not a tinkle. What's your name?

Torchie You'll twig it soon, Mr Flood. I'm sure you will!

Travis I doubt it.

Torchie Well, if you don't, you don't.

Slight pause.

You know what you being here has made me feel, Mr Flood?

Travis Haven't a clue.

Torchie Chosen. It's true! Now I know how Moses must have felt when he saw the burning bush. He must have looked at those flames and heard it jabbering away ten to the dozen, and he must have thought, Lor'struth!

Slight pause.

Why me?

Pause.

Travis *holds lilies out to* **Torchie**.

Travis You might as well have these?

Torchie But they were for Rio surely.

Travis You'll probably appreciate them more.

Torchie You always understood people so well, Mr Flood.

Travis It's nothing.

Torchie It's everything! If you don't mind me saying so. Gestures like this. Flowers from the heydays . . .

Slowly, **Torchie** *steps forward and takes flowers from* **Travis**. *She holds them as if they're priceless.*

Travis *starts idly brushing at the soot on his cuff again.*

Torchie Mr Flood – your cuff!

Travis What?

Torchie Your sleeve! That's not soot, is it?

Travis Yes. From the window-frame.

Torchie That's my fault. Telling you to look at the graveyard and not warning you of the soot. I could hang myself. I'll get a cloth.

Torchie *puts flowers on table, then goes to sink.*
She starts damping a flannel.

Travis Don't trouble yourself.

Torchie It's no trouble at all, Mr Flood. Here's you giving me flowers, and how do I repay you? I soil your beautiful clothes.

Torchie *returns to* **Travis** *with flannel.*

Torchie (*indicating one of the chairs*) Please. Sit down, Mr Flood.

Travis *takes step towards chair, then hesitates.*

Torchie Don't worry, the chairs have been thoroughly de-sooted.

Travis *sits.*

Torchie *tries to kneel beside him, but it's obviously both difficult and painful with her damaged leg.*

Travis (*getting to his feet*) Here! You sit. I'll stand.

Torchie I wouldn't hear of it, Mr Flood.

Travis But it's hurting you.

Torchie What I deserve. My punishment. Now . . . just got to get the drumstick in place.

Torchie *continues to settle herself. She yells out in pain a few times.* **Travis** *watches, getting increasingly agitated. With one last cry* **Torchie** *gets her leg settled.*

Torchie There!

Slowly, **Travis** *sits again.*
Torchie *starts dabbing at* **Travis**'s *cuff.*
Travis *looks round at room.*

Torchie There was a terrible fire, Mr Flood.

Travis I can see that.

Torchie Almost a year ago now.

Slight pause.

One night . . . one night I woke up and . . . What are those flies called, Mr Flood? Flies that look like they're on fire.

Travis . . . Fireflies?

Slight pause.

Torchie One night I woke up and the air was full of fireflies. Lor'struth they were beautiful. Then one of the fireflies landed on my blanket. It turned into a flame. And I just lay there, Mr Flood. In a burning bed. Watching. The wallpaper caught fire. It turned to ash and floated in the air. That does look pretty, I thought. My face was tingling in the heat. My eyes were watering. But did I move? No. I just lay there, calmly watching the whole world burn up around me. And do you know something, Mr Flood? It was the most peaceful I'd ever been.

Pause.

I was lucky to get out alive.

Travis But you did, obviously.

Torchie Only because of Rio. She'd been woken by the fireflies as well. Only she had the sense to know what they were. Lor'struth, I might not be the sharpest knife in the dishwater, but even I should have twigged you don't get many fireflies in Bethnal Green.

Travis You got out safe and sound. That's the main thing.

Torchie Safe, yes. But not altogether sound, Mr Flood.

Torchie *touches her bandaged leg.*

Travis Ah, I see.

Torchie My dancing days were over anyway.

Travis Must have been very painful.

Torchie There were times I screamed 'Cut it off! I'd rather hop around than go through this!' A terrible time. But you know who helped me through it all, don't you?

Travis Who?

Torchie Rio, of course.

Travis Of course.

Torchie She looks after me, Mr Flood. She's the
breadwinner.

Travis I'm well aware of that.

Torchie We have to live! If it wasn't for Rio, we'd be on the
streets. Oh, I know what some people think. And I know it
would never have happened in the heydays. Believe me, I
never thought I'd end up living like this. But sometimes you
have no choice. I love Baby Rio and Baby Rio loves me. She
might be a little rough and ready on the outside, but inside
she's got a heart of gold.

Slight pause.

Travis I'm sure she has. A heart of pure gold. Just like her
grandmother.

Torchie Thank you, Mr Flood.

Travis And her mother, I have no doubt.

Torchie (*flinching*) Oh . . .

Slight pause.

Travis What?

Torchie *begins to get up.*
Once more, it causes her pain.
Travis *goes to help.*

Torchie (*sharply*) Don't help . . .

Finally, **Torchie** *gets to her feet.*
She takes flannel back to sink.

Torchie You touched a heartache just then, Mr Flood. A
great heartache.

Slight pause.

Travis Your daughter?

Torchie My Donna, yes. My beautiful Donna. Rio's mother. Do you remember her?

Travis No.

Torchie She adored you when she was a child, Mr Flood.

Travis I have a way with children.

Torchie I'll say you did, Mr Flood. Me and Donna were down Bethnal Green Road market one day. She must have been . . . oh, six at the time. And, lor'struth, was she crying. You know the way children get. Crying for no reason other than the need to make tears. I bought her some popcorn. She loved popcorn, my Donna. Always smelt of it.

Travis Popcorn was her perfume.

Torchie You remember!

Travis . . . No.

Pause.

Torchie You appeared, Mr Flood. Just as much a vision then as you are now. And you saw my crying Donna and you looked so sad. You took the white lily from your lapel and you gave it to her. Instantly, her crying stopped. Then you got in your car and drove away, as if it was the most natural thing in the world for you to end the heartache of children. Oh, I treasured that flower, Mr Flood. Like it was a splinter from the Cross itself.

Pause.

Travis I gave my lilies to lots of people.

Torchie You did?

Torchie *sits opposite* **Travis**.

Travis *glances at his wristwatch.*

Pause.

Torchie Well, perhaps it's best that you can't remember Donna. You'd be so upset if you knew what happened to her.

Pause.

It was terrible.

Pause.

I see a bruise.

Travis A bruise?

Torchie A bruise on my Donna. But not a normal sort of bruise. Lor'struth, no. If I tell you where it was, Mr Flood, perhaps you can guess what kind of bruise it is.

Torchie *touches her neck.*

It's here!

Slight pause.

Travis . . . A lovebite?

Torchie A lovebite it is, Mr Flood.

Travis How old is she?

Torchie Well, she's no longer the six-year-old girl you gave the lily to, Mr Flood. That was in the beginning of the heydays. No, we're at the end of the heydays now. Nineteen sixty-nine. And, although my Donna might still have her hair in a pony-tail and smell of popcorn, she's fourteen years old. And she's standing in front of me – in this very room – with a lovebite on her neck. She's trying to hide it under her blouse collar . . . but there it is! 'Who did that, Donna?' I ask. She doesn't want to tell me. 'Is it someone at school . . . All right, all right! Don't get in a mood. Just make sure your Dad doesn't see it. He'll hit the roof if he does and kill the boy to boot. And I hope you're not doing anything silly – Where are you going? Don't storm into the bedroom! I haven't finished with you yet!' But I don't pry any more, Mr Flood. I've got to allow her some privacy, haven't I? It's only a lovebite. No harm in it. I won't ask any more questions.

It's the right thing to do, don't you think, Mr Flood? Tell me it's the right thing to do!

Travis Yes, it's right.

Torchie Wrong!

Slight pause.

It's a few months later now, Mr Flood. I'm waiting for my Donna to come home from school. Quarter past four. She should be here any minute. I start making tea. Half past four. She's probably chatting with a friend. She's very sociable. Five o'clock.

Torchie *starts pacing the room.*

She's never been this late before, Mr Flood. Not without telling me. Lor'struth, she knows how I worry. I'm imagining all sorts of things.

Torchie *goes to window.*

There's no sign of her, Mr Flood! 'Donna! Donna!' Half past five. I know something's wrong, Mr Flood. What shall I do? If I go out to look for her, she might come back while I'm out. Or, if there has been an accident, the police might come. I'm a nervous wreck . . . And then the door opens. 'Where have you been, you naughty girl! It's nearly six o'clock. I'm out of my mind with worry . . . What's wrong? . . . You went to see the doctor? But, why, Donna? What's wrong with you . . .' And what does she tell me, Mr Flood. What words come out of her mouth?

Travis She's pregnant!

Torchie I should have asked more questions when I saw the lovebite. 'Donna, you've got to tell me who the boy is . . . He's responsible. He's got to pay.' But she won't tell me, Mr Flood. She's crying. I stroke her hair. And all I'm thinking is, how am I going to tell Mr Sparks.

Travis Mr Sparks?

Torchie My husband. He's a religious man, Mr Flood. He can quote the Bible and often does. And he adores little

Donna. She's his little angel. He's standing there, Mr Flood.
By the window. 'Now calm yourself!' He starts trembling.
'We've got to help our Donna!' He's going very red. 'No!
Leave her alone!' He's hitting Donna, Mr Flood. 'Stop it!
Stop it! She won't tell you the boy's name! I've asked her a
million times! Stop!' He's beating her black and blue! Her
nose is bleeding. Stop him, Mr Flood! Stop him! Stop him!

Travis Stop!

Pause.

Has he stopped?

Torchie Yes, Mr Flood. It's later now. We're discussing
what to do! We have no idea. Our little girl pregnant. The
father unknown. Oh, what can we do?

Travis Abortion.

Torchie We could never have allowed that, Mr Flood. Not
in the heydays. We've just got to go through with it. Donna
will have the child. We won't press to find out who the boy
is. Mr Sparks will pray to God to forgive his sinning
daughter. And everything will work out all right in the end!
Right, Mr Flood?

Travis Right!

Torchie Wrong!

Slight pause.

(*Suddenly flinching.*) Lor'struth!

Travis (*startled*) What is it?

Torchie Can't you hear it?

Travis What?

Torchie Screaming! Coming from in there!

She indicates bedroom.

There it is again!

Travis It's Donna?

Torchie She's having the baby, Mr Flood. Sooner than we thought.

Torchie *approaches bedroom.*

'Shush, Donna! Don't worry! Mummy's here!'

Torchie *looks into bedroom.*

Oh, she's bleeding! Blood everywhere. What shall I do, Mr Flood?

Travis Where's Mr Sparks?

Torchie He's not here!

Travis Get a doctor!

Torchie And leave Donna alone! Another scream! I'm going to panic, Mr Flood.

Travis Don't panic.

Torchie Tell me what to do?

Travis Boil some water!

Torchie Good idea. But it does no good.

Travis What do you mean?

Torchie The screams, Mr Flood. Can't you hear them? They're getting louder and louder.

Torchie *rushes into bedroom.*

Pause.

Travis Wh . . . what's happening?

Torchie A baby girl, Mr Flood. My Donna's given birth to a beautiful baby – Ahhhhh!

Travis What is it?

Torchie She's dead, Mr Flood!

Travis What? The baby?

Torchie (*impatiently*) Lor'struth! Not the baby, Mr Flood.

Torchie *enters.*

How can it be the baby? She grew up to meet you in the graveyard this afternoon. Now pay attention!

Torchie *goes back into bedroom.*

Slight pause.

Travis It's your daughter.

Torchie *enters, looking stricken.*

Torchie My Donna was too good for this place, Mr Flood.

Travis She was.

Torchie The good die young.

Travis They do.

Torchie *and* **Travis** *sit.*

Pause.

Torchie I called the baby Rio. Donna always liked Westerns, you see.

Travis Very good.

Torchie And I've brought up Baby Rio all by myself. She reminds me of Donna in so many ways. The way she smiles. Or threads her fingers together.

Pause.

Did you ever have any children, Mr Flood?

Travis No. But I can imagine that losing –

Torchie No, you can't. Only a parent can imagine what losing a child must be like. You see, your child is everything, Mr Flood. It's your future. When I lost my daughter . . .

Travis Don't think about it. It's over.

Torchie I've spent a lifetime thinking about it. It will never be over.

Torchie *looks down, upset.*

Travis You'll make me cry if you cry.

Torchie (*looking up, forcing a smile*) Lor'struth, Mr Flood. I've done all my crying. No tears left. I'm as dry as a desert where that's concerned. Besides, you haven't come back after all these years to hear my heartache.

Travis If it helps you to burden me, I don't mind.

Torchie I mind.

Slight pause.

Shall I tell you something funny?

Travis That would be a relief.

Torchie Look around.

Travis What?

Torchie Just look!

Travis *looks round.*

Torchie Now if you can remember my name, you'll have a bit of a chuckle.

Travis Your name's Sparks.

Torchie You remember!

Travis No.

Torchie Then how – ?

Travis You told me your husband's name was Mr Sparks.

Pause.

But it is funny. The Sparks family living in a burnt house. Very droll.

Torchie I've got a sense of humour haven't I, Mr Flood?

Travis No one has the ability to laugh at their misfortunes like the women of the East End.

Torchie And I bet you've met lots of women, Mr Flood.

Travis Some of the most glamorous in the world. But they bore me. And you know why? No humour. Something goes wrong – a car crash or some minor disfigurement – and it's nothing but long faces and feeling sorry for themselves. But you! Not a bit of it. Your whole world falls to pieces and you still crack a joke. I tell you I'd rather look at your legs and hear your sense of humour, than look at their million-dollar legs and listen to their humourless drivel any day. It's a privilege to have your humour to entertain me. And that's no exaggeration, Mrs Sparks –

Torchie Oh, you never called me Mrs Sparks.

Travis I didn't.

Torchie Lor'struth, no.

Travis What did I call you then?

Torchie By my nickname. Like everyone else. You'd call it out every Saturday night. Remember?

Travis No.

Torchie You will.

Travis I won't.

Torchie You might.

Travis Just tell me. We haven't got all night.

Torchie True. But we've got until my granddaughter turns up.

Pause.

Travis I want to show you something.

Travis *takes a paperback book from his pocket.*

Torchie A book.

She peers closer.

With your name on it!

She peers closer still.

'The Man with the White Lily.' Lor'struth, Mr Flood. That's you! You were the man with the white lily.

Travis I've written the story of my life. It's why I've come back. To do some publicity. See the photograph on the back?

Travis *shows* **Torchie** *back cover of book.*

Torchie Oh . . . Mr Flood! A heyday you! In your black suit and tie. And the lily, of course. Pure pizzazz.

Travis (*offering book to her*) Have a good look.

Torchie *hesitates a moment, then wipes her hands on her dress and takes the book almost reverentially.*

She sighs and stares at photograph for a moment.

Torchie All the girls used to swoon over you, Mr Flood. You were their flame.

Travis I know.

Torchie *opens book.*

Torchie 'Chapter One. I was born . . .' You don't waste much time, do you, Mr Flood. Straight in the deep end. Just like you.

Flicks through the pages.

Oh, look! The heyday church!

Flicks page.

And the heyday pub!

Flicks page.

The heyday market! Where I used to shop. Where you gave Donna that lily. I used to get my cheese and ham there. And there . . . there's the butcher's. I was in there one day when you walked in, Mr Flood. You didn't see me. Why should you? The shop was full. And of course, there was no queuing for you. 'Here comes Mr Flood', people said. And we parted like the Red Sea. You were with two of your boys. They had black suits on. Just like you. There you stood. In the middle of the butcher's, looking at all the meat. Then you pointed at half a cow hanging from a meathook. Sawn clean in half it was, its insides showing and everything. You snapped your fingers and your two boys took the carcass down. Blood was still dripping everywhere. Your boys carried it out of the butcher's and threw it in the back of your car. There was blood all over their suits. And across the pavement. But none on you.

Slight pause.

Travis What a memory you have.

Torchie Any second of the heydays is more real to me than anything that's happened since. When I think of the heydays it's like thinking of . . . of another place. Does that sound foolish? I suppose it does. But I can't help it. The heydays are like a perfect place for me. A perfect place I visited once, but can never visit again.

Long pause.

Torchie *goes to give book back to* **Travis**.

Travis Keep it.

Torchie Keep it?

Travis A gift.

Torchie Lor'struth, Mr Flood. Where will your generosity end.

Torchie *clutches book to her chest.*

Will you do something for me, Mr Flood?

Travis If I can.

Torchie Will you sign it for me?

Travis Delighted.

Travis *takes book.*

Pause.

Knowing your name might help.

Slight pause.

Torchie Every Saturday night you'd visit. And every Saturday night you'd see me and call, 'Evening, Torchie!'

Travis Torchie! That's your nickname?

Torchie *nods.*

Travis I'm glad we've got that over and done with.

Torchie You still don't remember me though, do you, Mr Flood?

Travis Not a thing.

Travis *signs book.*

'To Torchie. Yours, Travis Flood.'

Travis *hands* **Torchie** *book.*

Torchie I'll worship it. This and the lilies – The lilies! Lors'truth! I best put them in some water.

Torchie *puts book on table, then gets vase from cupboard and fills it with water.*

I've got some serious arranging to do. I used to love flowers in the heydays.

Torchie *takes vase over to table and spreads flowers out.*

Mr Sparks used to buy me flowers for my birthday.

Travis How long has he been dead?

Torchie Who?

Travis Your husband.

Torchie Mr Sparks isn't dead, Mr Flood.

Travis But you said . . . I'm sure you said you brought your granddaughter up all by yourself.

Torchie I did.

Torchie *goes to drawer and removes a pair of extremely large silver scissors.*
She holds them in the air, snipping them.

Torchie Scissors!

Torchie *goes back to flowers and starts trimming the stalks.*

Pause.

Oh, no, Mr Sparks is not dead.

Torchie *continues snipping stalks.*

Slight pause.

Travis He left you, then?

Torchie No. He didn't leave me.

Pause.

Torchie *continues snipping stalks.*

Travis So what happened?

Torchie Oh, you don't want to keep hearing my heartache.

Travis I do.

Pause.

Torchie Praying!

Travis Praying?

Torchie That's what I can hear, Mr Flood. Mr Sparks praying. He hasn't stopped since the day Donna was buried. I try to help him, but what can I do? I have a baby to look after. I have no time to grieve. But for Mr Sparks, grief is all he has. I've heard of the phrase 'mad with grief' but I've never seen it until now. It breaks your heart to see him.

Travis Where is he?

Torchie Sitting over there by the window. See him? Staring at the night sky. See him?

Travis Yes.

Torchie And he's praying, Mr Flood. Endless whispered prayers.

Travis I hear him.

Torchie 'You've got to pull yourself together. Baby Rio needs us. Donna is dead. There's nothing we can do about that! And – lor'struth – your praying is giving me a headache!' He's mumbling something now. 'What's that? . . . A comet? . . . Where?'

Torchie *goes to window and looks out.*

'No. I can't see a comet!' But he can, Mr Flood. He can see it blazing over Bethnal Green. And, suddenly, he's up, Mr Flood! He's rushing out! He's rushing to the roof. I want to run after him. But Baby Rio is crying! She's screaming! What shall I do, Mr Flood? Run after Mr Sparks or comfort Baby Rio? Baby Rio might be choking! What shall I do, Mr Flood? Tell me! Tell me!

Travis Comfort the baby!

Torchie Thank you, Mr Flood. Here I am! Rocking her in my arms. 'Shush now, Baby Rio.' She stops crying. There! It was the right decision, wasn't it, Mr Flood? To comfort Baby Rio and not run after Mr Sparks? Right?

Travis Right!

Torchie Wrong! Because it's while I'm rocking Baby Rio I hear the crash. Something has fallen from the roof, Mr Flood. Will you look out of the window and tell me what you can see.

Travis *hesitates.*

Torchie I can't go! I've got the baby in my arms.

Slowly, **Travis** *gets up.*
He goes to window and – being careful of the soot – looks out.

Travis It's Mr Sparks?

Torchie Yes, Mr Flood. He tried to kill himself.

Travis But he's not dead?

Torchie No.

Travis Injured?

Torchie It was his brain, Mr Flood. The hospital did what they could. But . . . but he's like a child now, Mr Flood. Stares at me with wide, empty eyes. And he just mumbles and gurgles. He hasn't said a word I've understood in twenty-five years.

Travis He's been in hospital for twenty-five years!

Torchie I visit him every night! Where I was going when you turned up.

Slight pause.

Travis That last year of the heydays everything changed. It was a bad year for me.

Torchie For you! What about *me*, Mr Flood! Imagine what it was like for me! At the beginning of the year I was happy. I had a husband, a daughter, all I ever wanted. By the end of the year my daughter was dead, my husband little more than a vegetable, and a baby granddaughter to bring up single-handed. Oh, yes, for me the heydays were well and truly over.

Torchie *stares at flowers in vase.*

Long pause.

Torchie (*softly*) Did I do something, Mr Flood? Was I being punished for some sin?

Travis I try not to think like that.

Torchie It's hard not to sometimes.

Pause.

Travis Torchie?

Torchie Mr Flood?

Travis Why don't you put the kettle on. I'm gasping for a cup of tea.

Torchie Of course, Mr Flood. Lor'struth, I should have offered you one earlier. Whatever will you think of me?

Torchie *puts kettle on.*

She starts getting cups, milk, sugar, tea-bags, etc.

Travis It's been years since I've had a traditional East End cuppa.

Torchie Well, we'll soon put that right.

Slight pause.

Travis I tell you what, Torchie. I could just murder some bickies if you've got any.

Torchie I should have.

Torchie *gets packet of biscuits.*
She finds it almost empty.

Torchie Oh, look at this! Rio and her friends have been at them. They're like a plague of locusts those girls. Only two left. I hope that's enough for you, Mr Flood.

Torchie *puts both biscuits by* **Travis**.

Travis (*giving* **Torchie** *back a biscuit*) We'll have one each, Torchie.

Torchie (*giving* **Travis** *back the biscuit*) You asked for them.

Travis (*giving* **Torchie** *the biscuit*) One is fine.

Torchie (*giving* **Travis** *the biscuit*) But you're hungry.

Travis (*giving* **Torchie** *the biscuit*) Not that hungry.

Torchie (*giving* **Travis** *the biscuit*) It's only fair.

Travis (*giving* **Torchie** *the biscuit*) It's not fair at all.

Torchie (*giving* **Travis** *the biscuit*) You're the guest, Mr Flood –

Travis (*angrily, giving* **Torchie** *the biscuit*) Just have a bloody bicky!

Torchie *tenses and stares at* **Travis**.

Long pause.

The kettle boils.

Torchie *finishes making tea and gives* **Travis** *a cup.*

Then she sits at table with her cup.

They both dunk biscuits in the tea.

Very long pause.

Travis Can I ask you something, Torchie?

Torchie What?

Travis Have I aged much?

Torchie Not really.

Travis I watch my waistline.

Torchie Good for you.

Travis Twenty lengths a day.

Torchie Twenty lengths?

Travis Of my swimming-pool.

Torchie In your own backyard no doubt.

Travis My own hundred-foot garden, Torchie.

Torchie Oh, don't, Mr Flood!

Travis Had the pool built myself. To my own design. 'It'll cost a fortune,' they said. 'We'll have to uproot those palm trees and dig up that cactus.' 'Well, you just start uprooting and digging,' I told them, 'because I want to be floating on a Lilo and sipping pina colada by the end of the month.'

Torchie I had a pina colada once.

Travis You strike me as a pina colada sort of woman.

Torchie That's one of the nicest things anyone's ever said to me.

Travis Then your life's been short of nice things.

Torchie It has, Mr Flood. Did they finish your pool in time?

Travis Naturally. They knew I meant business. I'm not a man to mess with when my mind's set on something, as well you know, Torchie. Now I float and sip in the most beautiful pool in all Hollywood.

Torchie Hollywood?

Travis Where I live now.

Torchie Must be heaven.

Travis Near as damn. I'll tell you my typical day, shall I? A day in heaven with Travis Flood. I wake up. What do I feel? Silk sheets! What do I see? Golden sunlight coming through the windows. I get up, then take my breakfast out to the poolside –

Torchie You don't make your own breakfast surely.

Travis No . . . My butler does that. Then I have a swim. Sip those pina coladas you like to get drunk on, Torchie. Then I get dressed and cruise about in my black Cadillac.

Torchie You always liked black cars.

Travis Where shall I go today? The mountains? The beach – ?

Torchie The beach! If it's not too far.

Travis *mimes driving car.*

Travis No distance in this car. Best suspension in the world.

Torchie Hardly know you're moving.

Travis Notice the palm trees. And yellow sand as far as the eye can see.

Torchie Can we sunbathe?

Travis That's dangerous, Torchie. Sun-rays give you cancer.

Torchie Daylight didn't harm us in the heydays, did it, Mr Flood?

Travis Put this sunblock on and we'll go shark fishing in my boat.

Torchie Shark fishing!

Travis I'll put some bait on the fishing-hook.

Travis *mimes putting bait on hook.*

Torchie What do you use, Mr Flood?

Travis Steak.

Torchie Steak! I'd never have thought sharks had a taste for steak. Not many cows in the ocean, after all, are there?

Travis Anything bloody will do.

Pause.

Travis Not boring you, Torchie!

Torchie Haven't had such a good time in years.

Slight pause.

Travis I've got something! Good God, it's a big one! There! Torchie! You see it?

Torchie Where?

Travis There! The shark! Jumping in and out of the ocean.

Torchie It's huge! Don't let it get away!

Travis I won't! Come here, you devil!

Torchie Pull, Mr Flood!

Travis It's coming! Look at the jaws!

Torchie So many teeth.

Travis There! On the deck. Be careful, Torchie. It's still alive.

Torchie What a monster!

Travis Watch it die!

Torchie and **Travis** *watch the imaginary shark in front of them.*

Torchie *is becoming worried and uncomfortable.*

Travis What is it, Torchie?

Torchie It's suffering, Mr Flood.

Travis Won't be long now.

Torchie But its fin's all a-quiver. It's in pain . . . Oh . . . the poor thing . . . Throw it back, Mr Flood!

Travis What about dinner? You can have shark steaks!

Torchie I'd rather have a rissole! Please! Mr Flood! Before it's too late.

Torchie *is becoming increasingly agitated.*

Travis All right, all right.

Travis *throws imaginary shark back into the ocean.*

Travis There! There it goes.

Torchie I want to go home now.

Travis Yes, go home.

Torchie I want to sit by the swimming-pool.

Travis We'll watch the sunset.

Torchie Then go to bed.

Travis What do you feel?

Torchie Silk sheets.

Slight pause.

Travis And that, Torchie, is my day in heaven.

Pause.

Torchie Life's been good to you, Mr Flood.

Travis It has.

Torchie Someone up there likes you.

Travis They must.

Torchie No heartache for you.

Pause.

Travis No.

Pause.

Torchie To think . . . you're one of our own made good.
You don't mind me saying that, do you?

Travis I'm proud of it. When people ask me where I'm from
I don't say 'England' or 'London', I say, 'I'm a Bethnal
Green lad born and bred.' I haven't lost my accent, have I?

Torchie Not at all!

Travis I practise it! Every day!

Slight pause.

Can I tell you something, Torchie? I might have everything
a heart desires, but sometimes . . . sometimes I'm lonely.
Lonely for this place. And salt of the earth people like
yourself.

Travis *lifts cup.*

To the heydays.

Torchie (*lifting cup*) To the heydays.

Travis *and* **Torchie** *clink cups and drink some tea.*

Pause.

Travis *reaches out and gives* **Torchie**'s *hand a squeeze.*

Torchie *is visibly moved.*

Pause.

Torchie Mr Flood, I'd like to show you something.

Travis What, Torchie?

Torchie I don't usually show anyone. But tonight . . . for . . . you . . . Mr Flood, will you look the other way? And don't look round till I tell you. Will you do that for me please?

Travis *looks the other way.*

Torchie *goes into bedroom.*

Travis Mind if I smoke, Torchie?

Torchie (*from bedroom*) It's hardly likely to bother me after my house nearly burnt down, is it now, Mr Flood?

Travis You have a remarkable way of looking at things, Torchie.

Travis *takes a large cigar from his pocket.*
He lights it with a gold lighter.

Travis I hope Rio appreciates what a remarkable grandmother she has.

Torchie *reappears.*

She has an old-fashioned cinema serving-tray around her neck and is holding a torch: cinema usherette items from the 1960s.

She goes to the main light-switch and turns light off.

Torchie You can look now, Mr Flood.

Travis *turns.*

Torchie *lights up her serving-tray.*
It is very bright.

Torchie Can I see your ticket please?

Travis (*laughing*) Well, look at this. Ha-ha. Look at you, Torchie. Torchie!

Torchie Smoking or non-smoking, sir?

Travis (*laughing*) Oh . . . er . . . smoking, I guess.

Torchie This way, sir.

Torchie *switches her torch on.*

*It shines directly into **Travis**'s eyes.*

Travis (*dazzled, still laughing*) Lor'struth, Torchie.

Travis *rubs his eyes.*

Torchie *is walking round the room, as if showing someone to their seat in the cinema.*

Torchie (*calling*) Cigarettes! Ice-cream! Programmes!

Travis *stops laughing.*

He is looking troubled now.

He watches **Torchie**.

Torchie *notices* **Travis**'s *expression.*

Torchie What is it, Mr Flood?

Travis N . . . nothing.

Torchie Lor'struth, you look like you're going to faint. You better sit down.

Torchie *helps* **Travis** *to his seat.*

Travis I remember!

Torchie You remember!

Travis Everything!

Torchie Me and my husband.

Travis You ran the local cinema!

Torchie The Empress, yes. And you remember my little Donna?

Travis Donna! The girl from the cinema! It was *her*! Oh, my God! It was her!

Torchie I know, Mr Flood. It gets me that way sometimes – And look! Here!

She takes a pressed flower from the tray.

It's the lily you gave my Donna. All those years ago. Pressed flat as paper. Still with us.

Torchie *holds flower out to* **Travis**.

Pause.

Then, very slowly, **Travis** *takes flower.*

He stares at it, horrified.

Torchie *sits and watches* **Travis**.

Pause.

Torchie Those days mean as much to you as they do to me, don't they, Mr Flood? I ran back into the flames to save these few things. But – lor'struth – they were worth getting a drumstick for. You understand that, don't you, Mr Flood?

Pause.

Travis Torchie . . .

Torchie Yes, Mr Flood?

Travis I did . . . things. During the heydays. Things I'd . . . forgotten.

Torchie I forget some things too –

Travis That's not what I meant! The things I did . . . I . . . I forget them because . . . I had to forget.

Torchie Had to?

Travis I made myself forget.

Torchie I'm not sure I understand you, Mr Flood.

Slight pause.

Travis Torchie . . . seeing you like this. How it all went wrong for you. From that one . . . terrible thing. What happened to your daughter . . .

Torchie I understand you now, Mr Flood.

Travis You can't.

Torchie But I do. You're trying to say you should have stopped it in some way.

Travis Stopped it?

Torchie You were there to protect us.

Travis . . . Yes.

Torchie And you should have prevented what happened.

Travis Oh, yes.

Torchie But you mustn't think that way, Mr Flood.

Travis I mustn't?

Torchie No. You see, this is what I believe. We don't get away with anything in this life. Everything has to be paid for. So, whoever was responsible for what happened to my Donna will get his punishment. And I hope he shrieks in agony for all the suffering he's caused.

Pause.

Travis So much lost, Torchie.

Pause.

Torchie We don't lose anything, Mr Flood. Not really. One day I was sitting here when I felt a chill. I came out in goose bumps. Goose bumps so big you could hang your hat on them. Someone's just walked over my grave, I thought. And then . . . then I could smell her. Like burying my head in her clothes. Popcorn! And I knew, Mr Flood. Knew my Donna was in the room with me.

Travis *stares at* **Torchie**.

Pause.

Torchie Everything was very quiet, Mr Flood . . . And then . . . then I saw something . . . Hazy mist. And the mist took shape. Arms, legs, a white dress . . . It was the ghost of my Donna, Mr Flood.

Pause.

She spoke to me.

Travis What did she say?

Torchie That she was happy.

Travis Nothing else?

Torchie That's all I needed.

Slight pause.

From that day on, Mr Flood, I've been able to call her to me. I just say her name. And, if I say it with every bit of love in my heart, she comes back. Like a daughter should. Let me call her now, Mr Flood. So you can speak to her.

Travis I . . . well, I don't believe in ghosts so –

Torchie Donna!

Travis Don't!

Torchie Too late! Can't you feel? The chill?

Pause.

Travis (*softly*) Yes.

Torchie (*showing her arm*) Goose bumps! And you too, Mr Flood. I can see them.

Travis Can't you stop her?

Torchie (*shivering*) Someone's just walked over my grave.

Slight pause.

Torchie *sniffs.*

Popcorn!

Travis *stands.*

Torchie Donna, Mr Flood has returned to visit us. And look
. . . Here's the lily he gave you.

Torchie *holds the pressed lily out in front of her.*

Torchie She's almost here, Mr Flood.

Long pause.
Very still and silent.

Suddenly . . . the door crashes violently open.

Rio Sparks *enters.*

Rio *is twenty-five years old and strikingly beautiful. Her long,
platinum blonde hair is tied in a pony-tail and she is heavily made up:
smooth, heavily powdered pale complexion, lots of eye-liner, and bright
red lipstick. She is wearing a roughly made, golden cheerleaders' outfit,
and boots (painted gold), and is holding a baseball bat. Her nails are
very long and varnished gold. There is a tattoo of a heart on her left
arm.*

She is chewing gum.

Both **Travis** *and* **Torchie** *scream out at her entrance.*

Torchie Lor'struth, Rio!

Rio *turns the main light on.*

Rio *and* **Travis** *look at each other.*

Torchie *continues clutching at her heart.*

Torchie You scared me to death!

Rio (*at* **Torchie**) Holy Smoke! Sorry, Mighty Gran.

Rio *helps* **Torchie** *sit, then takes the serving-tray off her and puts it
on the table.*

Torchie My heart's going to explode.

Rio It won't explode.

Torchie It will if you keep opening the door like that.

Rio Come on, Mighty Gran. Let's get you ready for the hospital.

Torchie They'll be taking me there on a stretcher one of these days.

Rio Don't fuss, Mighty Gran. (*At* **Travis**.) You're early, Travis.

Torchie Baby Rio! You can't call him by his first name. Don't you know who it is?

Rio 'Course I know.

Torchie Then a little respect if you please.

Rio (*at* **Travis**) You don't mind if I call you Travis, do you, Travis?

Travis . . . No.

Torchie Mr Flood, please –

Rio Now, come on, Mighty Gran. On your way or you'll be late. Grandad Sparks'll be wondering where you've got to. I'll get your coat.

Rio *picks up usherette tray from table.*

Torchie Mr Flood bought the flowers, Baby Rio. He gave them to me but they were meant for you.

Rio Flowers for me! That's a laugh!

Rio *goes into bedroom with tray.*

Torchie It proves he's a gentleman, Baby Rio. A gentleman from the heydays.

Rio If he was a gentleman, he wouldn't be here in the first place.

Travis *is still staring after* **Rio**, *transfixed.* **Rio** *enters with black coat.*

Rio Here we are, Mighty Gran.

Torchie Doesn't Mr Flood look smart.

Rio (*helping* **Torchie** *on with coat*) He does, Mighty Gran.

Torchie He lives in Hollywood now. Got his own swimming-pool. A black Cadillac. Speedboat. He's even written a book about his life. See? He's very rich. I'm sure he'll be very generous. You hear me?

Rio Loud and clear, Mighty Gran.

Rio *hands* **Torchie** *the walking-stick then urges her towards the door.*

Rio Now get on your way.

Torchie (*at* **Travis**) You can stay till I get back if you like, Mr Flood.

Rio Give Grandad Sparks a kiss for me.

Torchie Mr Flood?

Rio (*firmly*) Goodbye, Mighty Gran.

Torchie She's got a heart of gold really, Mr Flood –

Rio (*almost pushing* **Torchie** *out of the house*) 'Bye!

Rio *closes door behind her and stares at* **Travis**.

Pause.

Rio You can finger me, lick me, fuck me. You can spunk on me anywhere you like from my neck down. Smudge my make-up or mess my hair and I'll cut your nuts off. I'll finger your prostate, lick your balls and suck your cock. You can watch me wank. Or I'll watch you wank. You can do anything in front of me except piss or shit. That stuff's too smelly. No choking or cutting either. Apart from that I'll do most things. All right, let's get started. Take your clothes off.

Travis *is just staring at* **Rio**.

Travis What . . . what are you?

Rio What do you mean, what am I? I'm the thing you want to fuck.

Rio *takes a step towards* **Travis**.

Travis *steps back.*

Rio What's wrong with you? You look like you've just seen a ghost. I'm no ghost, Travis.

She grabs his right hand and puts it on her breast.

Feel that! Oh, yes, that's turning me on! You certainly know how to please a woman, don't you, Travis. Holy Smoke!

Travis *is staring at* **Rio** *with a look somewhere between horror and amazement.*

Rio *reaches for his flies.*

Rio Let's see what you got!

Travis *pushes himself free.*

Rio You best stop playing games if you want to get your money's worth, Travis.

Travis I . . . I want to talk to you.

Rio Say anything you like. I get wet very easily.

Travis No . . . I want you to talk to me.

Slight pause.

Rio (*seductively*) I'm getting very juicy, Travis. I can feel it –

Travis That's not what I meant! I want you to tell me things about . . . about your life.

Rio I live in a burnt-out dump and I have to fuck ancient fossils like you for money! What do you think my life's fucking like? Now we going to get on with it or what?

Travis I can't.

Rio What do you mean, you can't? You were salivating over the tombstones this afternoon.

Travis Something's changed.

Rio You pay me even if we don't do anything!

Travis I've never paid!

Rio Then it's time you did.

Rio *reaches for* **Travis***'s pockets.*

Travis *pushes* **Rio** *aside. He takes a few steps towards door.*

Rio *grabs baseball bat.*

Rio Travis!

Travis *stops, halfway between door and* **Rio**. *He turns to face* **Rio**.

Rio If you try to get away without paying me, I'll fucking brain you. And then I'll get the rest of my gang. They're waiting for me in the graveyard. One scream from me and they'll be over here like bats out of hell. And we'll hurt you, Travis. Hurt you real bad.

Travis *makes tentative move towards door.*

Rio *raises baseball bat.*

Travis *hovers between* **Rio** *and door.*

Pause.

Travis *makes slight move towards door.*

Rio *raises baseball bat more threateningly.*

Rio What's it going to be, Travis? The decision's yours.

Travis *makes another move towards door.*

Rio *steps towards* **Travis**.

Travis *stops.*

Pause.

Suddenly, **Travis** *makes up his mind.*

He rushes for door.

Rio *lunges after him and strikes* **Travis** *with the baseball bat just as he's about to open the door.*

Travis *turns to face her, staggers back into room, falls to his knees.*

Travis I'm . . . Travis Flood!

Rio *strikes him again.*

Travis *collapses unconscious.*

Rio *is panting with excitement.*

Travis *is gently moaning.*

Rio *stands astride him.*

She lets out a piercing shriek.

The shriek is echoed deafeningly loud.

Blackout.

Act Two

Travis *is tied to a chair with lengths of golden brocade.*

Rio, Miss Sulphur *and* **Miss Kerosene** *are lined up.*

Miss Sulphur *is eighteen;* **Miss Kerosene** *is twelve. Like Rio, they are dressed in roughly made, golden cheerleader outfits, have long platinum blonde hair in pony-tails, long nails, varnished gold, and tattoos of hearts on their left arms. Their make-up is more extreme than* **Rio***'s, almost ghoulish. All three of them are chewing gum. They are collectively known as* **The Cheerleaders.**

The Cheerleaders *burst into a cheerleading chant the moment the lights come up. It is roughly choreographed, but what they lack in precision they make up for in energy.*

Gradually, though, **Miss Kerosene** *starts making more and more mistakes. She says the wrong words, steps on* **Miss Sulphur** *'s toes, etc.*

Cheerleaders
Cheer girls, sneer girls,
wrapped in golden gear girls.
Leer girls, queer girls,
the spread a little fear girls.

Glam girls, wham girls,
the just don't give a damn girls.
Sleek girls, freak girls,
the totally unique girls.

Flooze girls, cruise girls,
the we got no taboos girls.
Boot girls, cute girls,
with a liking to pollute girls.

C-H-E-E-R-L-E-A-D-E-R-S!
Cheerleaders!

Before the end of the routine – due to **Miss Kerosene** *'s persistent errors – everything has collapsed into chaos.*

Rio Holy Smoke, I give up.

Miss Sulphur *slaps* **Miss Kerosene** *round the head.* **Miss Kerosene** *looks at* **Rio** *for support, but* **Rio** *is looking at* **Travis**.

Travis *has been watching, laughing more and more.*

Travis If you think I'm threatened by you, you're wrong. I'm Travis Flood. I was theatening people before you were born. Crowds used to part to let me through. People brought me presents to keep me in a good mood. If I so much as sneezed I'd receive get-well cards by the lorry load. People would lick my boots and wipe my arse and consider themselves lucky to have that privilege. I'm Travis Flood! When I raised my voice the whole of East London would collectively shit itself. A snap of my fingers meant kneecaps would fly. And now you expect me to be scared by you? Bimbos dressed in kitchen foil –

Miss Sulphur Now wait a fucking minute! I'll allow you the bimbos. We're bimbos and proud of it. Someone say 'Amen!'

Miss Kerosene Amen.

Miss Sulphur But you insult a girl's togs at your peril. That's blasphemy.

Miss Kerosene Blasphemy!

Miss Sulphur Right, Miss Sparks?

Rio It's not important.

Miss Sulphur Not important! But he's insulting our image –

Travis Image! You don't know what the word means. An image should have style. Sophistication. In the heydays I had my suits made by the finest tailors on Saville Row. I had pizzazz. Where's the pizzazz in kitchen foil –

Miss Sulphur Listen to him.

Miss Kerosene Heretic!

Miss Sulphur Miss Sparks made these togs –

Miss Kerosene Amen!

Miss Sulphur With her own fair hands –

Miss Kerosene Amen –

Miss Sulphur (*shouting at* **Miss Kerosene**) Quit fucking 'Amening', will you!

Slight pause.

Travis I never had to shout at my boys. I always felt shouting was a sign of weakness. Mind you, it must be difficult to look strong in the first place when you're wearing . . . kitchen foil.

Miss Sulphur (*at* **Rio**) Listen to him! Miss Sparks, do something! (*At* **Travis**.) What's wrong with you? You want us to hurt you or what? Don't you realise just how much trouble you're already in? Try to mess with Miss Sparks.

Miss Kerosene Sin on top of sin!

Miss Sulphur Miss Sparks here is one mean-spirited girl. I've seen her do things with those nails of hers you wouldn't believe.

Travis She looks harmless to me.

Miss Sulphur She'll tear your fucking face off.

Travis In the heydays I would have –

Miss Sulphur You were a big fish in a small pond. That's all. Tell him, Miss Sparks! But now that pond's a cesspool. It's spawned mutant creatures like us.

Miss Kerosene Amen!

Miss Sulphur Tell him, Miss Sparks!

Miss Kerosene Tell him!

Miss Sulphur What did you do in your precious heydays anyway? Threaten shopkeepers? Shoot the odd nuisance in the head? That's nothing! Most kids have done that by the time they leave school these days. Tell him, Miss Sparks!

Miss Kerosene Tell him!

Miss Sulphur The worst you could have done is the height of good manners to us, Little Gangster –

Travis Don't call me gangster!

Miss Kerosene *gets very close to* **Travis**.

Miss Kerosene (*slowly and deliberately*) Little Gangster!

Travis *spits in* **Miss Kerosene***'s face.* **Miss Kerosene** *and* **Miss Sulphur** *gasp in shock. They stare at* **Rio**.

Miss Sulphur (*at* **Rio**) You going to let him get away with that? You just going to stand there while he spits in our faces – (*At* **Travis**.) I hope for your sake you haven't damaged Miss Kerosene's make-up. (*At* **Miss Kerosene**.) Let me have a look, girl.

Miss Sulphur *looks at* **Miss Kerosene***'s face.*

Miss Kerosene Lipstick?

Miss Sulphur Check!

Miss Kerosene Powder?

Miss Sulphur Check!

Miss Kerosene Eye-liner?

Miss Sulphur Check! No damage done, girl. (*At* **Travis**.) Smudging someone's make-up is a sin. Tell him, Miss Sparks! It's breaking a commandment. One of the commandments of the Cheerleaders. He should learn, Miss Sparks! Tell him! You should learn, Little Gangster –

Travis Don't call me gangster!

Rio Oh, shut up!

Rio *takes handkerchief from* **Travis***'s top pocket and shoves it into his mouth.*

Travis *struggles but to no avail.*

Miss Sulphur *and* **Miss Kerosene** *whoop and cheer.*

Miss Sulphur *gets length of gold brocade and ties it round*
Travis'*s mouth, gagging him firmly.*

Rio Let's tell him the ten commandments, girls! (*Pointing at*
Miss Sulphur.) First, Miss Sulphur.

Miss Sulphur Always wear make-up!

Rio (*with* **Miss Kerosene**) Amen!

Miss Kerosene (*with* **Rio**) Amen!

Rio (*at* **Miss Kerosene**) Second, Miss Kerosene.

Miss Kerosene Be blonde!

Rio (*with* **Miss Sulphur**) Amen!

Miss Sulphur (*with* **Rio**) Amen!

Rio (*at* **Miss Sulphur**) Third!

Miss Sulphur Maintain a healthy pony-tail!

Rio (*with* **Miss Kerosene**) Amen!

Miss Kerosene (*with* **Rio**) Amen!

Rio (*at* **Miss Kerosene**) Fourth!

Miss Kerosene Keep bodies hard!

Rio (*with* **Miss Sulphur**) Amen!

Miss Sulphur (*with* **Rio**) Amen!

Rio (*at* **Miss Sulphur**) Fifth!

Miss Sulphur Wear gold togs!

Rio (*with* **Miss Kerosene**) Amen!

Miss Kerosene (*with* **Rio**) Amen!

Rio (*at* **Miss Kerosene**) Sixth!

Miss Kerosene Be tattooed!

Rio (*with* **Miss Sulphur**) Amen!

Miss Sulphur (*with* **Rio**) Amen!

Rio (*at* **Miss Sulphur**) Seventh!

Miss Sulphur Piss on men!

Rio (*with* **Miss Kerosene**) Amen!

Miss Kerosene (*with* **Rio**) Amen!

Rio (*at* **Miss Kerosene**) Eighth!

Miss Kerosene Dominate!

Rio (*with* **Miss Sulphur**) Amen!

Miss Sulphur (*with* **Rio**) Amen!

Rio (*at* **Miss Sulphur**) Ninth!

Miss Sulphur Celebrate the ruins!

Rio (*with* **Miss Kerosene**) Amen!

Miss Kerosene (*with* **Rio**) Amen!

Rio   (*at* **Miss Kerosene**) Tenth!

Miss Kerosene *hesitates, her mind a blank. She shoots* **Rio** *a pleading look.*

Rio Pray to –

Miss Kerosene Pray to Saint Donna!

Miss Sulphur Saint Donna was the mother of Miss Sparks. Betrayed by a man! She's now a saint in the Queendom above. Saint Donna, the Patron Saint of all damaged girls living in the ruins. We pray to her every day.

Pointing at **Miss Kerosene**.

And the prayer goes? Miss Kerosene. Go on! How does the prayer go?

Pause.

She's fucking forgot again!

Rio Patience, girl. Miss Kerosene? How does the prayer to Saint Donna go?

Pause.

Miss Kerosene Our . . . Saint Donna, who art in the Queendom . . .

Rio Good.

Miss Kerosene . . . Golden be thy name in the ruins as it is in the Queendom . . . Deliver us from men . . . and . . . and . . .

Rio Encourage our sins –

Miss Sulphur Don't keep helping her.

Rio Why not?

Miss Sulphur She should know it.

Miss Kerosene I do know it.

Miss Sulphur Say it then!

Miss Kerosene Encourage our sins and . . . and –

Miss Sulphur She doesn't fucking know it!

Miss Sulphur *approaches* **Miss Kerosene**.

Miss Sulphur Encourage our sins as we forgive no one that sins against us. For thine is the Queendom. The make-up and the pony-tail. For ever and ever. Amen.

Miss Kerosene (*weakly*) Amen.

Miss Sulphur (*hitting* **Miss Kerosene**) Don't forget again.

Miss Kerosene (*at* **Rio**) She's always hitting me.

Miss Sulphur You deserve it. (*At* **Rio**.) Right, girl?

Pause.

Rio I've got more important things to worry about.

Rio *approaches* **Travis** *and starts prowling round him.*

Miss Sulphur Go for it, girl! Go for it!

Miss Kerosene Hurt him!

Rio Oh, I will, Miss Kerosene. But not yet. After all, suffering is measured by how long it lasts.

Miss Sulphur Amen to that, girl.

Miss Kerosene Amen!

Rio *continues prowling round* **Travis**. **Travis** *watches her, warily.*

Miss Kerosene *sits at table and starts blowing bubbles, watching eagerly.*

Rio (*picking up book from table*) Seen this, Miss Sulphur?

Miss Sulphur What is it, Miss Sparks?

Rio Story of his life, Miss Sulphur.

Miss Sulphur Well, lordy-lordy, Miss Sparks.

Miss Kerosene Hit him with it!

Rio No.

Opens book.

Chapter One. 'I was born in a paradise on earth called Bethnal Green – ' You must be fucking joking, Little Gangster. Paradise? This place. Don't think we'd say that, would we, Miss Sulphur?

Miss Sulphur Certainly wouldn't, Miss Sparks.

Rio What do you think, Miss Kerosene?

Miss Kerosene No way, Miss Sparks.

Rio Our stories are different to yours, Little Gangster. You wanted to know the story of my life! So now you're going to get it! Listen! The story of Rio Sparks. Chapter One . . . I was born in that room there. My mother was fourteen years old. There was a lot of blood. She didn't complain. Just bit her lip and squeezed me into the world. Behold, Rio Sparks!

Miss Sulphur Praise be!

Miss Kerosene Praise be!

Rio My mother was buried. Grandad went mad with grief. Tried to kill himself. And Rio . . . she was brought up by Mighty Gran. The most wonderful and loving woman ever to walk the ruins.

Miss Sulphur Amen to that.

Miss Kerosene Amen.

Slight pause.

Miss Sulphur *approaches* **Rio.**

Rio Chapter Two.

Miss Sulphur *stops.*

Rio Mighty Gran didn't have much money. Couldn't even afford Rio a bag of crisps. Rio dreamed of her mother.

Slight pause.

Miss Sulphur You done well, girl.

Miss Sulphur *approaches* **Rio.**

Rio Chapter Three.

Miss Sulphur *stops.*

Rio At the age of nine Rio was stealing from shops. Little gifts for Mighty Gran. At school she got into fights. With boys and girls. Rio never lost a fight. One day she fights off five boys, all of them older than her –

Miss Kerosene You told me eleven!

Rio It was only five.

Miss Kerosene But you said –

Rio Five is the truth!

Pause.

Rio Chapter Four. Rio stops going to school. She's hit a teacher by now and they're glad to see the back of her. She prowls the streets. Looks at crumbling buildings.

Miss Sulphur Drunks in the gutter.

Miss Kerosene Dumps.

Miss Sulphur Graffiti.

Rio And she thinks, this is where I belong. I'll dominate the ruins!

Miss Kerosene The eighth commandment!

Rio Chapter Five –

Miss Kerosene Or is it the ninth? Is dominate the same as celebrate –

Rio Don't push it, Miss Kerosene!

Pause.

Chapter Five. People on the streets become afraid of Rio. They point her out. Rio likes it. She likes being noticed. Her nails get longer. She wears more and more make-up. Men start lusting after her. Rio doesn't mind. She visits old men in dingy flats. They finger her and suck her nipples. Tell her she's the most beautiful thing in all the ruins. They cry with the pleasure of touching her skin. Rio laughs and takes their money. One old git refuses to cough up. Rio's claws flash in the darkness. Rio steals everything he has then kicks him hard in the balls.

Miss Sulphur Serves him right!

Rio Amen, Miss Sulphur!

Miss Kerosene How come she can say something and I can't?

Miss Sulphur Because you're a stupid arsehole and I'm not.

Rio Stop it, you two! You hear me? Just stop it! How can I tell things properly with you two bickering away?

Miss Sulphur *and* **Miss Kerosene** *stare at* **Rio**.

Slight pause.

Rio Chapter Six. One day Rio sees a boy. He's wearing a leather jacket. Rio likes what she sees. She wants it. She –

Miss Sulphur Not the boy.

Rio What?

Miss Sulphur Not the boy. Tell it our way, Miss Sparks. It's not the boy you like. It's the leather jacket.

Miss Kerosene That's what you always told me.

Miss Sulphur Because that's the way it was, Miss Kerosene. Miss Sparks saw the boy. And she liked his leather jacket. So she . . . she follows the leather jacket. All she's thinking about is getting that jacket. She's so fucking blinded by the leather jacket she doesn't realise she's walked straight into a dark alley. And what's in the alley? The boy's fucking gang, that's what! They attack Miss Sparks. Miss Sparks fights back. She claws at the boy's face. The boy gasps. There's blood in his spit –

Rio I'll tell this! This is my story!

Slight pause.

There are two other members in the boy's gang. They grab hold of Rio. There's lots of kicking and punching. It hurts. Rio's scared –

Miss Sulphur But she doesn't let them see that!

Rio She's screaming in pain and fear.

Miss Kerosene Kick them in the balls.

Rio Rio's weak now. Her legs are giving way. The boy with the jacket grabs a bottle. He smashes it. Brings it close to

Rio's face. 'I'm going to cut you bad,' he says. Rio feels the jagged glass against her skin –

Miss Sulphur And then she hears a voice!

Miss Kerosene Yes!

Miss Sulphur 'Leave her alone!' it says.

Miss Kerosene Her saviour!

Miss Sulphur And I rush forward!

Miss Kerosene Holding a baseball bat!

Miss Sulphur Swinging it through the air, Miss Kerosene!

Miss Kerosene Brain the boys!

Miss Sulphur I do.

Miss Kerosene Crack heads open!

Miss Sulphur I do.

Miss Kerosene Beautiful! Beautiful!

Miss Sulphur The boys are unconscious in the rubble.

Miss Kerosene Hope they rot.

Miss Sulphur Rio and her saviour go to the canal to bathe their wounds.

Miss Kerosene Their minor wounds!

Miss Sulphur Sitting by the canal. Looking up at the stars. I ask, what's your name?

Rio . . . Rio Sparks.

Miss Sulphur Miss Sparks! So call me . . . Miss Sulphur!

Miss Kerosene Miss Sparks and Miss Sulphur! Together at last!

Miss Sulphur Together for ever!

Pause.

Chapter Seven. Rio tells Miss Sulphur about her mother. They visit Donna's grave. They kneel beside it.

Slight pause.

Miss Sulphur (*pointing up*) Look! The clouds are swirling in the sky. Moving together. They're . . . they're making a shape. It's . . . it's a girl! A fourteen-year-old girl with blonde hair tied in a pony-tail. A miracle! You know what this means? Your mother is a saint!

Miss Kerosene Praise be!

Miss Sulphur Amen! She's a saint in heaven. All her suffering was not in vain. It means something. Don't you see that, girl?

Rio . . . Yes.

Miss Sulphur I give you that meaning. Ain't that right, girl?

Rio . . . Yes.

Miss Sulphur And we start to worship Saint Donna. Make up a prayer for her –

Miss Kerosene (*eagerly*) Saint Donna, who art in –

Miss Sulphur We don't need to hear it!

Miss Kerosene But I remember it now. Miss Sparks, I do –

Miss Sulphur (*hitting* **Miss Kerosene** *hard*) Shut up!

Miss Kerosene *starts choking on her chewing-gum.*
She spits her gum out.

Miss Kerosene (*holding chewing-gum up*) You nearly fucking choked me to death!

Miss Sulphur Good!

Miss Kerosene It's not fair. I can't do a thing right in this gang.

Miss Sulphur So leave.

Miss Kerosene I . . . I don't want to –

Miss Sulphur Why not?

Miss Kerosene I've got nowhere to go. I want to stay. You can hit me if you want.

Miss Sulphur *(thoughtfully)* Well . . .

Rio Don't torment her. (*At* **Miss Kerosene**.) You're a Cheerleader. Stay.

Pause.

Miss Kerosene *puts chewing-gum back in mouth and starts blowing bubbles.*

Rio Chapter Eight. Miss Sparks and Miss Sulphur are happy together. They steal, hurt, threaten, get drunk, take drugs and generally sin.

Miss Sulphur Happy times.

Rio *doesn't react.*

Pause.

Miss Sulphur Happy times?

Pause.

Rio And then Rio meets the boy in the leather jacket again.

Miss Sulphur I'd forgotten about him.

Slight pause.

Tell it, then.

Rio Chapter Nine. The boy's face has been badly scarred by Rio's nails. She can't believe her hands could do so much damage. She touches the boy's face. The skin is so soft. Rio and the boy . . . they begin to see more and more of each other. At first they meet secretly. Then they don't care. Walk along the streets with their arms round each other. Rio likes being held by the boy. Feels safe . . . He strokes my hair, whispers things. I feel his breath against my –

Miss Sulphur He's just using you.

Slight pause.

Rio Miss Sulphur doesn't like the boy.

Miss Sulphur He just wants you for a cheap fuck, that's all. He doesn't care for you. Not like I do. Do you think he does?

Rio I don't know.

Miss Sulphur Do you think he can protect you like I can?

Rio . . . I . . .

Miss Sulphur Choose! It's him or me.

Pause.

Rio (*softly*) You.

Miss Sulphur What?

Rio (*louder*) You!

Miss Sulphur Kiss me, Miss Sparks.

Rio *doesn't move.*

Slight pause.

Slowly, **Miss Sulphur** *approaches* **Rio**. *She holds* **Rio** *in a tight embrace and kisses her.*

Rio *pushes* **Miss Sulphur** *away.*

Rio Chapter Ten. The boy dies.

Pause.

He kills himself. Miss Sulphur doesn't care. She's happy. Laughs. Later, she persuades Rio to go to the boy's grave and cover it in graffiti –

Miss Sulphur You wanted to do it! It was golden graffiti! It was fun!

Rio Chapter Eleven. Rio smells smoke.

Slight pause.

Rio wakes up and jumps out of bed. Sparks everywhere. 'Mighty Gran!' she cries. 'Mighty Gran!' Rio saves her. But Mighty Gran's leg is badly burnt. She lays in hospital crying with the pain. Rio holds Mighty Gran's hand. But Mighty Gran, she never complains. She is strong and brave.

Miss Sulphur Amen to that.

Rio (*at* **Miss Sulphur**) Say 'Amen' all you like. Don't change anything. (*At* **Travis**.) You know why the house caught fire, Little Gangster? Because the boy's gang set fire to it, that's why. Because of what we did to his gravestone. The gold graffiti. That's why Mighty Gran suffered, still suffers, will always suffer. (*At* **Miss Sulphur**.) Because of what you made me do!

Pause.

Miss Sulphur Anything else you want to say? Any Chapter Twelve?

Pause.

Rio I . . . I find this gold material . . . I make the clothes. We name ourselves the Cheerleaders. And that's it. Nothing left to tell.

Pause.

Miss Sulphur You forgot Miss Kerosene. How could you? Poor Miss Kerosene. She's one of us. Hasn't she got a story to tell.

Miss Kerosene That's right! I have!

Miss Sulphur Don't worry, Miss Kerosene. Miss Sulphur hasn't forgotten about you. Even if Miss Sparks has. I know you've got a story.

Slight pause.

Miss Kerosene appears in the ruins. She –

Rio Let her tell it.

Miss Sulphur What?

Rio It's her story. Let her tell it. Chapter Thirteen. Miss Kerosene's story.

Miss Kerosene *tries to find the words.*

Pause.

Miss Sulphur Go on, then. You've been butting in all fucking night. Let it rip, girl.

Slight pause.

Miss Kerosene Don't know what to say.

Pause.

Miss Sulphur (*at* **Rio**) You see? I'll tell it —

Miss Kerosene Chapter Thirteen. I'm twelve years old. I ran away from home. I liked it on the streets. Ate food from dustbins. Drank rainwater. When I wanted to feel happy I sniffed glue . . . Saw beautiful things. One day I saw millions of insects fly out of the sky. Large black things with hairy legs. They landed on everything. On the cars, on the buildings. I caught one and squeezed it between my finger and thumb. It exploded yellow puss all over my face. I licked it off. Tasted like . . . honey!

Pause.

And then, one day, I saw two golden creatures walking through the ruins. They were magnificent. Said they called themselves the Cheerleaders. I wanted to be part of them. I asked, Can I join you?

Rio What's your name?

Miss Kerosene What's yours?

Rio Miss Sparks.

Miss Sulphur Miss Sulphur.

Miss Kerosene So call me . . . Miss Kerosene!

Rio (*at* **Miss Kerosene**) I think you belong with us. Don't you, Miss Sulphur?

Miss Kerosene You do?

Rio *and* **Miss Sulphur** *nod.*

Rio But first . . . we'll have to do something. Right, Miss Sulphur?

Miss Sulphur What?

Rio The tattoo.

Miss Kerosene What tattoo?

Rio Tell her, Miss Sulphur.

Miss Sulphur The red heart of Saint Donna.

Rio It needs to go on your arm.

Miss Kerosene How will you do it?

Rio Tell her, Miss –

Miss Sulphur Stop telling me what to do!

Slight pause.

We'll do it with this needle and ink.

Miss Kerosene (*bravely*) Go ahead!

Rio That's not what you said.

Miss Kerosene It's not?

Rio You know it's not. We're being honest now, girl. Tell her again, Miss Sulphur.

Miss Sulphur . . . We'll have to tattoo you.

Slight pause.

Miss Kerosene (*timorously*) How will you do it?

Rio The needle.

Miss Kerosene But it'll hurt.

Miss Sulphur It's supposed to fucking hurt.

Miss Kerosene Then I don't want it.

Miss Sulphur Do you want to be part of the gang or not?

Miss Kerosene Yes . . . but –

Miss Sulphur Then you get tattooed.

Miss Sulphur *and* **Rio** *grab* **Miss Kerosene**.
Miss Sulphur *stabs* **Miss Kerosene**'*s arm with the imaginary
needle.*

Miss Kerosene (*struggling*) Ahhh . . .

Miss Sulphur Hold her tight, Miss Sparks.

Miss Kerosene Ahhh!

Miss Sulphur *continues stabbing at* **Miss Kerosene**'*s arm.*

Miss Kerosene'*s screams turn to a whimper.*

Rio It'll soon be over! Don't worry. There! All finished.

Miss Kerosene Let me see!

Miss Kerosene *looks at tattoo on arm.*

Rio *strokes* **Miss Kerosene**'*s hair affectionately.*

Rio You're a Cheerleader now!

Rio, **Miss Sulphur** *and* **Miss Kerosene** *embrace. Then* **Miss
Kerosene** *detaches herself and approaches* **Travis**.

Miss Kerosene I'm a Cheerleader. I sparkle by night and
glitter by day. The ruins are my domain. Nothing will ever
harm me again. I've got battery acid in my veins –

Travis *claps slowly.*

Miss Kerosene Hang on! Look! His fucking hands are
untied!

Travis *takes the gag from his mouth.*

Travis They were never tied properly in the first place.

Miss Sulphur (*at* **Miss Kerosene**) Tie him up! (*At* **Travis**.)
What game you playing, Little Gangster?

Travis You don't seem to be able to do anything right –

Miss Sulphur *strikes* **Travis** *hard round the head.*

Rio Don't!

Miss Sulphur *glares at* **Rio**.

Miss Sulphur And why, pray tell?

Pause.

Travis Because . . . it's her job to hurt me. Right, Rio?

Miss Sulphur Call her Miss Sparks.

Miss Sulphur *hits* **Travis** *again.*

Rio Don't! You heard!

Slight pause.

It's my job.

Travis *and* **Rio** *stare at each other.*

Miss Kerosene *has been tying* **Travis***'s hands and thoroughly checking the remaining brocade that binds him.*

She now feels something in **Travis***'s jacket pocket and removes three cigars.*

Miss Kerosene (*holding cigar in air*) Cigars!

Miss Sulphur Could do with one of those, girl.

Miss Sulphur *takes two cigars from* **Miss Kerosene** *and gives one to* **Rio***.*

Miss Kerosene *reaches in* **Travis***'s pocket. She finds lighter and lights her cigar.*

Miss Kerosene *hands lighter to* **Miss Sulphur***.*

Miss Sulphur *lights her cigar, then hands lighter to* **Rio***.*

Rio *lights cigar.*

Pause.

Rio *approaches* **Travis***.*

Pause.

Rio *takes lily from* **Travis***'s lapel. Slowly, she burns lily with lighter.*

Miss Kerosene *and* **Miss Sulphur** *watch, transfixed.*

Travis *watches also.*

Pause.

Travis Is that supposed to hurt me in some way?

Miss Sulphur You're not doing your job, girl.

Travis None of you are. You threaten, but do nothing. In the heydays, we knew how to hurt –

Rio I know how to hurt.

Travis Burning flowers doesn't count. It's what you do to skin that matters.

Miss Kerosene I've done bad things to skin.

Travis I've done worse.

Miss Kerosene What's the worst thing you've done?

Travis My secret.

Miss Kerosene Tell us.

Travis Never.

Rio If I hurt you enough, you'll tell.

Travis Ah, at last! Now we're getting somewhere. Go on! You've got the cigar! Do it! I dare you.

Pause.

Slowly, **Rio** *loosens* **Travis**'s *tie. Then she undoes the top few buttons of his shirt and pulls it open, exposing his chest.*

Miss Kerosene *is giggling.*

Miss Sulphur *is watching* **Rio**.

Pause.

Very slowly, **Rio** *takes a drag on the cigar.*
Its tip glows very bright.

Then, slowly, she brings the tip of the cigar close to **Travis**'s *chest.*

Pause.

Rio *burns* **Travis** *with cigar, then backs away.*

Miss Kerosene's *giggles get louder.*

Travis Oh, you'll have to do better than that.

Slight pause.

Slowly, **Rio** *approaches* **Travis***, then burns him again.*

Rio Tell.

Travis Make me!

Rio *backs away from* **Travis** *and stares at him.*

Slight pause.

Rio (*at* **Miss Kerosene**) Burn him!

Miss Kerosene *rushes in to burn* **Travis** *with cigar.* **Travis** *cries out.*

Rio (*at* **Miss Sulphur**) You too!

Miss Sulphur *rushes in to burn* **Travis***, then stands back.*

Slight pause.

Rio Again!

Miss Kerosene *and* **Miss Sulphur** *rush in to burn* **Travis***. After each burn they back away to look at their handiwork.*

Rio Tell.

Travis Make me!

Rio *burns* **Travis***, then backs away, watching.*

Slight pause.

Rio (*at* **Miss Kerosene** *and* **Miss Sulphur**) What you waiting for?

Miss Kerosene *and* **Miss Sulphur** *rush in, frantically burning* **Travis***.*

Rio *joins in.*

Miss Kerosene (*burning* **Travis**) Tell!

Miss Sulphur (*burning* **Travis**) Tell!

Rio (*burning* **Travis**) Tell!

Rio, **Miss Sulphur** *and* **Miss Kerosene** *back away.*
They are a little breathless now, getting excited by the attack. There is a slight lull as they look at **Travis**.

Rio (*screaming*) More!

Rio, **Miss Sulphur** *and* **Miss Kerosene** *continue burning* **Travis**.

Miss Kerosene *is giggling.*

Miss Sulphur *is panting, watching* **Rio**.

Rio *is getting more and more frantic.*

Travis *is screaming.*

But they still burn him, carried away by the frenzy of it all.

The attack is savage and protracted.

Rio *stubs her cigar out on* **Travis***'s neck. She is almost uncontrollable now.*

Miss Sulphur You're losing it, girl! That's enough.

Rio That's for me to say.

Miss Sulphur But he's learnt his lesson.

Miss Sulphur *snatches cigar from* **Rio**.

Travis That's nothing, Rio! Nothing!

Rio *looks round for something else to hurt* **Travis** *with.*
She sees scissors, picks them up and raises them in the air.

Miss Kerosene Look at her!

Miss Sulphur What you doing, girl?

Miss Sulphur *and* **Miss Kerosene** *back away from* **Rio**. **Rio**
spreads blades of scissors and raises them in the air. Then – very, very slowly – she approaches **Travis**. *She is aiming blades at his face.*

Miss Kerosene She's going to do it!

Miss Sulphur It's too much, girl!

Rio *gets closer to* **Travis**.

The scissors' blades get closer to his face.

Then . . . just as **Rio** *is about to attack* **Travis** *. . .*

Travis It's Saturday night!

Rio *freezes.*
Pause.
Then **Rio** *goes to strike with scissors again.*

Travis I'm wearing my black suit.

Rio *freezes again.*
Slowly, she calms.
She lowers scissors.

Rio Let's hear it then. It's Saturday night. You're wearing
your black suit. Go on.

Travis There's a lily in my lapel. I always wear a lily. I'm
the man with the white lily. I look immaculate. I'm with my
two boys. They're wearing black suits too. We're out
collecting money. That's what we do every Saturday night.
I'm standing in front of a large building. Can you see it?
There's neon lights. Very bright. It's the last stop of the
evening. A cinema.

Travis*'s words are beginning to touch nerves in* **Rio** *now.*

Miss Sulphur *watches* **Rio**, *aware of her reactions.*

Travis I go to the projection room. That's where the man
works. It's him I get the money from. Look! There! The
projector is showing a film. Flickering light everywhere. And
here's the man. Standing in front of me. He's looking
nervous. Face covered with sweat. 'What's that? You haven't
got all my money. Shut up! Don't give me excuses! I'll hurt
you, you fucking bastard!' My boys grab hold of him now.
They're twisting his arm. The man's screaming. 'I'll break
your arm if you try to fuck with me!' He's begging me to
stop. 'You don't mean anything to me.' Look at him! He's on
the floor now. One of my boys kicks him. 'Next week you pay
me twice, you fucking shit! If not I'll – '

Travis *looks round as if catching sight of something.*

Someone's walked into the room. It's the man's daughter.
She's looking at me. Those large eyes. Let go of him! The girl
rushes up to her dad. 'Don't worry. He's not hurt bad. Not
yet.' I walk out of the projection room. My boys are
following me. We leave the cinema and go up to the car. And
then – I see those eyes again. 'What do you want? Speak up,
I can hardly hear you. Why am I hurting your dad? Well
. . . why don't you get in the car and I'll tell you.' My boys
are laughing. They know what's on my mind. 'Keep watch
you two! Now . . . get in the car.' Oh, the girl is so beautiful.
She has long blonde hair in a pony-tail. She's getting in the
car.

Her name is . . . Do you know her name?

Rio Donna!

Miss Kerosene What's going on? I don't get it! He's
supposed to be telling us the worst thing he ever did.

Miss Sulphur He is. He did it to Saint Donna.

Miss Kerosene You mean he . . . he's the one who –

Miss Sulphur Lordy-lordy, Little Gangster.

Miss Kerosene I don't believe it!

Rio I believe it!

Miss Kerosene But that means . . . Fuck! (*At* **Rio**, *giggling*.)
He's your dad!

Rio (*at* **Miss Kerosene**) Get out!

Miss Kerosene What?

Rio Get the fuck out.

Miss Sulphur Do as she says, girl.

Rio (*at* **Miss Sulphur**) You too!

Miss Sulphur You don't mean that!

Rio I do.

Miss Sulphur But . . . this is me, girl. You can't do this to me! I made your life mean something. Don't forget all the things we've done. Miss Sparks and Miss Sulphur. Together for ever. The Cheerleaders –

Rio Out!

Slight pause.

Miss Kerosene (*at* **Miss Sulphur**) Don't upset yourself.

Miss Sulphur Upset? Me! Don't make me laugh. It takes more than this stupid cow to upset me. Listen to me, Miss Sparks, you were nothing when I first met you and you'll be nothing when I'm gone. I hope you rot. (*At* **Miss Kerosene**.) Let's go! This chapter's over!

Miss Sulphur *gives* **Travis** *one last look, then exits.*

Miss Kerosene *hesitates.*

Miss Kerosene We . . . won't see each other again?

Rio No.

Miss Kerosene Is it because I talk too much? Or . . . kept forgetting the prayer?

Rio It's not that.

Miss Sulphur (*off-stage, impatiently*) Miss Kerosene!

Miss Kerosene I've . . . got to go with her. There's nothing else.

Rio I know.

Miss Kerosene *backs towards door a little.*

Miss Kerosene We had good times.

Rio No, we didn't.

Miss Kerosene *exits.*

Rio *closes door behind her.*

Rio New Chapter. The truth.

Rio *sits opposite* **Travis.**

Rio We're in the car.

Travis Your dad owes me money. That's why I hurt him. What do you say to that?

Rio He . . . he can't afford to pay!

Travis Then he gets hurt some more. And so does your mum.

Rio No! Please!

Travis Maybe you can help.

Rio What is it? I'll do anything!

Travis Come closer, Donna.

Rio Will you stop asking them for money?

Travis Yes.

Rio And hurting them?

Travis Yes, yes.

Slight pause.

Rio What . . . what are you doing?

Travis Relax.

Rio It hurts!

Travis Shut up! Do you want me to hurt your mum and dad?

Rio No.

Travis Then do as you're told. And you mustn't tell anyone! You hear me? Not your mum or dad. No one –

Rio You're making me bleed.

Travis I'm kissing your neck.

Rio I'm crying.

Pause.

Afterwards I run out of the car. I'm hysterical –

Travis No! You're very calm. You walk back to the cinema. I watch you from the car. I'm waiting for you to look back. But you don't. Not once. You go into the cinema. The door swings shut behind you. I never see you again.

Rio I die.

Travis I never knew that. I'd run away by then. Left it all behind.

Rio You go to America.

Travis Yes.

Rio With your fortune.

Travis There is no fortune. There never was. I go there with nothing. And that's how it stays. No swimming-pool. No Cadillac. No speedboat. Just an endless succession of petty jobs. And always moving. And everywhere I go I change my name. Invent new stories about myself. In the end, I begin to forget who I am. Who I was. So I write a book . . . Yes! I wore a black suit! Crowds parted to let me through! A snap of my fingers meant kneecaps would fly! Yes! In a paradise called Bethnal Green they will remember, they will remember who I am . . . I have to publish the book myself. It costs me nearly everything I've got. The rest goes on a plane ticket and this suit. I'm the man with the white lily again. I come back here. Visit all my old haunts. But . . . hardly anybody remembers me. One old tramp laughs and says I look like a gangster. And that's it. Except . . . in a graveyard I meet a girl. We talk for a while. She says she's heard about me. We arrange to meet later. She gives me the address. But I arrive early. I talk to her grandmother. She tells me stories. And . . . I piece together another story. A story the grandmother's not even aware of. A story about me. Now I know who I am.

Pause.

And I'm sorry.

Pause.

Very slowly, **Rio** *stands.*
With scissors, she cuts the brocade from **Travis**'s *hands and feet.*

She puts brocade back in drawer.
Then, she goes to sink and dampens flannel.
She returns to **Travis** *and, with almost ritualistic slowness, cleans his*
face and neck.

She does the buttons up on his shirt and straightens his tie.

She returns flannel to sink.

Pause.

Rio *gets brush and brushes* **Travis**'s *hair until it looks presentable.*

She puts gold lighter back in his pocket.

Pause.

Rio *takes band from her own hair, freeing it from its pony-tail. Her*
hair falls over her shoulders.

Pause.

Rio That boy in the gang. I loved him very much. He killed
himself because I left him. I'm sure of that.

Slight pause.

We've both done terrible things.

Pause.

You best go before Mighty Gran gets back.

Travis Will you tell her?

Rio No.

Slowly **Travis** *stands.*
He makes his way to the door and opens it.

Rio Wait.

Travis *turns.*

Rio *goes to vase of lilies. She breaks off a flower, then puts it in* **Travis**'s *lapel.*

Slight pause.

Travis Thank you, Miss Sparks.

Rio You're welcome, Mr Flood.

Travis *exits.*

Slight pause.

Rio *starts tidying the room: straightening chairs, throwing away cigar butts, cleaning up burnt flower, etc. She's in the process of doing this when* **Torchie** *enters.*

Torchie Mr Flood gone, Baby Rio?

Rio Yes, Mighty Gran.

Torchie And you're doing some tidying up!

Rio Yes.

Torchie And your hair's different too!

Rio . . . Yes.

Torchie *is watching* **Rio** *intently, aware that something is different about her.*

Torchie Lor'struth, my leg aches.

Rio Sit down, Mighty Gran. I'll take your bandage off for you.

Torchie You'll – Lor'struth! What's come over you?

Torchie *sits.*
Rio *kneels in front of her and starts unbandaging* **Torchie**'s *leg.*

Rio How was Grandad Sparks?

Torchie About the same. I said to him, 'Guess who's back at our house? Mr Flood! Mr Flood back from the heydays.' I thought that might cause some reaction. But no! Nothing!

Lor'struth, I should have known better. Gave up on that years ago.

Pause.

So . . . was Mr Flood generous? Did he give you something special?

Rio . . . Yes, Mighty Gran.

Torchie I knew he would.

Rio *continues unbandaging leg.*
Torchie *looks at* **Rio**.

Pause.

Torchie *reaches out and strokes* **Rio***'s hair.*
Rio *looks up and smiles.*
Torchie *flinches as some more bandage is removed.*

Rio I didn't hurt your leg, did I, Mighty Gran?

Torchie Lor'struth, no, Baby Rio. It's almost healed now.

Rio *embraces* **Torchie**.

Torchie Lor'struth, Baby Rio.

Fade to blackout.

25959